The Moon's Big Adventure

CHRISTOPHER J. CILAURO

PAGE PUBLISHING, INC.
Conneaut Lake, PA

First originally published by Page Publishing 2021

ISBN 978-1-64701-172-7 (pbk)
ISBN 978-1-64701-272-4 (hc)
ISBN 978-1-64701-173-4 (digital)

Printed in the United States of America

To my parents, who have always supported me. They *"love me to the moon and back"* and support my dream of becoming a writer.

To my Nana and Papa, who always tell me how proud they are of me.

To my late grandma, who was so happy when I told her I was getting my book published.

To my aunt, uncle, and cousins who believe in me no matter what I do.

The moon is always in the sky, but you see it mostly at night. The other half of the time, the sun is in the sky. During the day, while the sun is out, everybody is happy, smiling and having fun. But when it is nighttime and the moon comes out, everybody is sad that the fun is over, and it is time to go to bed. Every day the moon would look down and see everybody having adventures, and he wanted to have fun and adventures of his own.

The moon went to the sun and said, "Hey, sun, what do you think about me taking a vacation?"

The sun started to laugh. "You take a vacation? You only work half of the day because the other half of the time I'm in the sky, and all you do is light up the night sky."

"Why are you so important and I'm not?" said the moon.

"Well, I make people smile. I am the sun.

I make everyone do fun stuff like play outside on vacation and swim in the pool."

The sun laughed out loud. "What do you do? Make people go to sleep? Well, if you want to go on vacation, I have no problem with that, but you must ask the boss."

"Wait, there is a boss?" said the moon.

"Yes. You didn't know about the boss?" said the sun.

"No, I didn't know," said the moon.

"Well, if you want to go on vacation and have your own adventure, you must speak to the boss."

"All right," said the moon, "I will speak to the boss. Who exactly is the boss?"

"Mother Earth, of course!" said the sun.

"Well, enjoy your day in the sky, because I'm going to visit Mother Earth so I can begin my adventure!"

So the moon ventured out to find Mother Earth.

"Mother Earth," said the moon, "I would like to ask if I can go on vacation?"

"A vacation? No, no, no, no! You are much too important to the night sky," said Mother Earth.

"The sun told me that all I do is make people go to sleep!"

"You are far more important than that!" said Mother Earth.

"Without you, the night sky would be dark. You light up the night sky and help ships find their way in the dark."

Mother Earth thought about it and then said, "Okay. You can go on vacation, but you must be back by nightfall so you can light up the nighttime sky. Got that?"

"Yes!" said the moon.

"All right, well, pack your bags because you are going on vacation!" said Mother Earth.

"Okay," said the moon, and off he went.

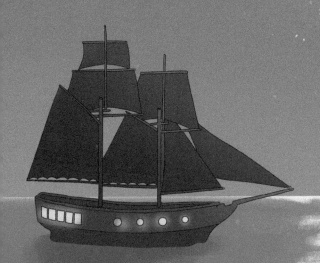

While he was packing his bag, he was thinking, *Where should I go to experience my adventure? I know, what about New York City? I hear there are always things to do there.*

So he finished packing his bag, and off he went.

When he arrived in New York City, he was filled with excitement. *What should I do first and where should I begin?* he thought.

He saw a few yellow cabs and said to a driver, "I am looking for adventure, and I have never been to New York City before."

"Well, hop right in," said the driver. "You have come to the right place!

Welcome to New York City! We have Broadway shows, the Empire State Building, the Statue of Liberty, Central Park, Time Square, and Fifth Avenue."

The moon said, "I want to see them all!"

The moon was having so much fun that he lost track of time and it became nightfall. How was he going to get back in time to light up the night sky? He looked up and saw how dark it was without his light in the night sky.

He saw how sad people looked walking around in the dark. So he hurried back because many people would be very disappointed and he would be letting everyone down.

He rushed back and made it on time to light up the night sky. The stars welcomed him back, and all was just as it should be in the night sky.

The moon had a great adventure. He realized that his job was much too important to take for granted because so many people depended on him.

The moon smiled and
glowed even brighter.

CPSIA information can be obtained
at www.ICGtesting.com
Printed in the USA
BVHW021920240521
608033BV00016B/723